The Boscombe Valley Mystery

Arthur Conan Doyle

About this Book

For the Student

🎧 Listen to the story and do some activities on your Audio CD
💬 Talk about the story
tune• When you see the orange dot you can check the word in the glossary
K Prepare for Cambridge English: Key (KET) for Schools

For the Teacher

 A state-of-the-art interactive learning environment with 1000s of free online self-correcting activities for your chosen readers.

Go to our Readers Resource site for information on using readers and downloadable Resource Sheets, photocopiable Worksheets and Answer Keys. Plus free sample tracks from the story.

www.helblingreaders.com

For lots of great ideas on using Graded Readers consult Reading Matters, the Teacher's Guide to using Helbling Readers.

Level 2 Structures

Past simple of *be*	Comparative
Past simple	Comparative with *as...as*
Past simple (common irregular verbs)	Superlative
Be going to	*To* for purpose
Past continuous	Adverbs of manner
Past simple v. past continuous	
	A lot of, not much, not many
Past simple in questions	And, so, but, because
Have to / must	Possessive pronouns
Mustn't	

Structures from lower levels are also included

Contents

	About the Author	6
	About the Book	7
	Before Reading	8
1	A telegram from Sherlock Holmes	13
2	The Boscombe Valley murder	16
3	James McCarthy's statement	20
4	We meet Miss Alice Turner	25
5	Holmes and Lestrade take the night train	29
6	Holmes is back with a story	32
7	Lestrade gets angry	34
8	Holmes follows the trail	37
9	A murderer's footprints	39
10	Holmes solves the mystery	44
11	Holmes asks Watson's advice	48
12	Mr John Turner speaks	54
13	A murderer's story	57
	After Reading	61

HELBLING DIGITAL

HELBLING e-zone is an inspiring new state-of-the-art, easy-to-use interactive learning environment.

The online self-correcting activities include:

- reading comprehension;
- listening comprehension;
- vocabulary;
- grammar;
- exam preparation.

- **TEACHERS** register free of charge to set up classes and assign individual and class homework sets. Results are provided automatically once the deadline has been reached and detailed reports on performance are available at a click.

- **STUDENTS** test their language skills in a stimulating interactive environment. All activities can be attempted as many times as necessary and full results and feedback are given as soon as the deadline has been reached. Single student access is also available.

FREE INTERACTIVE ONLINE TEACHING AND LEARNING MATERIALS

1000s of free online interactive activities now available for **HELBLING READERS** and your other favourite Helbling Languages publications.

ONLINE ACTIVITIES
www.helbling-ezone.com

blog.helblingreaders.com

NEW

Love reading and readers and can't wait to get your class interested? Have a class library and reading programme but not sure how to take it a step further? The Helbling Readers BLOG is the place for you.

The **Helbling Readers BLOG** will provide you with ideas on setting up and running a Book Club and tips on reading lessons **every week**.

- Book Club
- Worksheets
- Lesson Plans

Subscribe to our **BLOG** and you will never miss out on our updates.

About the Author

Sir Arthur Conan Doyle was the inventor of Sherlock Holmes, the world's most famous fictional• detective. Lots of people think Sherlock Holmes is a real person and write to 221B Baker Street, London, his address in Conan Doyle's stories!

Doyle was born in Edinburgh, Scotland in 1859. He worked as a doctor until 1891 but he had a passion for writing stories. In 1891 he decided to become a full-time writer. His first story was a novel called *A Study in Scarlet*. He then wrote a series of short stories called *The Adventures of Sherlock Holmes*, which were published in instalments• by *The Strand Magazine*. The public loved them, and wanted to read more about Sherlock Holmes and his faithful• friend, Dr Watson. *The Boscombe Valley Mystery* was one of these short stories. Conan Doyle wrote 56 Sherlock Holmes stories in total. One of the most famous and popular is *The Hound of the Baskervilles*.

In the end Conan Doyle became tired of writing about the detective and he decided to 'kill' his creation. In *The Final Problem* Holmes is murdered by his most dangerous enemy, Professor Moriarty. However, Conan Doyle's readers were so angry that in the end he decided to bring Holmes back to life in *The Empty House*.

Conan Doyle died in 1930. Sherlock Holmes's fictional house in Baker Street is now a museum.

Glossary

- **faithful:** loyal; good
- **fictional:** a person in an invented story is a fictional character
- **instalments:** the story is published in chapters or episodes

About the Book

The Boscombe Valley Mystery was first published as a short story in *The Strand* magazine in 1891. It then appeared in a book of short stories, *The Adventures of Sherlock Holmes*, in 1892. It appeared twice on British TV, in 1968 and 1991, and was also a play on the radio and in the theatre in 2007. It is interesting because it has a surprise ending.

The story begins when Dr Watson receives a telegram• from Holmes asking him to come to the west of England to help investigate• the Boscombe Valley murder.

The murdered man is Mr Charles McCarthy. His son James found him by the Boscombe Pool with injuries• to his head. He died a few moments later. People say Mr McCarthy and his son James had a big argument not long before this. The police put James in prison. But James says that he did not kill his father, and Holmes believes him. Miss Alice Turner, the daughter of Mr McCarthy's friend, believes James is innocent• and she asks Holmes for help to prove• this.

In the end Holmes proves that James McCarthy is innocent, and he also finds the real murderer.

- **injuries:** places on the body where people are hurt
- **innocent:** (here) did not do the murder
- **investigate:** find out information about
- **prove:** show
- **telegram:** paper with short message

Before Reading

🎧 **1** **Listen and match the descriptions to the characters. Label the pictures a to f.**

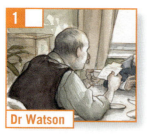
Dr Watson

Miss Alice Turner

James McCarthy

Inspector Lestrade

Sherlock Holmes

Mr John Turner

🎧 **2** **Listen again and answer the questions with the name of a character from Exercise 1.**

a) Who tells the story of the Boscombe Valley Mystery?
b) Who goes to the Boscombe Valley to help Inspector Lestrade?
c) Who believes that James McCarthy is the murderer?
d) Who is very beautiful and has blue eyes?
e) Who is in prison for the murder of his father?
f) Who is very rich but also very ill?

Before Reading

3 Match the words to the pictures.

telegram   prison   beard   magnifying glass   police   cloak

....

....

4 Use the words from Exercise 3 to complete the sentences below.

a) The famous detective Sherlock Holmes wears a hat and a long ....

b) He carries a .... with him.

c) Dr Watson receives a .... from Sherlock Holmes one morning.

d) James McCarthy is eighteen years old and in ....

e) The .... think James McCarthy murdered his father.

f) Mr John Turner is an old man with a long .... and grey hair.

9

Before Reading

1 **Listen and number the words in the order you hear them.**

☐ path ☐ grass ☐ pool ☐ gun ☐ farm ☐ woods

2 **Look at the picture. Match the things in the picture with the words from Exercise 1.**

Before Reading

3 Use the words from Exercise 1 to complete the sentences below.

a) On June 3rd, Mr McCarthy went to meet someone at the Boscombe Valley ....

b) Mr McCarthy left from Hatherley ....

c) He walked along a ....

d) There are .... on both sides of the pool.

e) While he was there his son James arrived with a ....

f) When James ran back, his father was lying on the ....

4 Read the sentences and put them in the correct order. Listen and check.

a) ☐ He had a big argument with his son James.
b) ☐ After 150 metres he heard a horrible sound.
c) ☐ Mr McCarthy went to the Boscombe Pool to meet someone.
d) ☐ He ran back and his father was lying on the grass.
e) ☐ He died a few moments later.
f) ☐ After the argument, James walked away.

5 Which of these is NOT a chapter in the story? Guess, then read the chapter names on page 3 to check.

a) A murderer's footprints
b) A telegram from Sherlock Holmes
c) Mr John Turner speaks
d) Holmes cannot solve the mystery

6 How much do you know about the famous detective Sherlock Holmes? Do you know any other Sherlock Holmes stories? Some of the stories are films or TV programmes, too. Which stories do you know? Say in your own words what happens.

1 A telegram from Sherlock Holmes

I am Dr Watson and I am a friend of the famous detective* Mr Sherlock Holmes.

One morning, my wife and I were having breakfast, when a telegram came. It was from Sherlock Holmes. He wrote:

> Dear Watson, Can you come and help me for a few days? Am going to the west of England to investigate* the Boscombe Valley murder. Please come. The Boscombe Valley is beautiful. We leave London from Paddington Station on the 11:15 train.

'What do you think?' said my wife, looking at me. 'Are you going to go?'

'Well,' I answered, 'I have a lot of patients* to see at the moment.'

'The other doctor can see your patients,' my wife replied. 'You can have a little holiday. You know you like to help Mr Sherlock Holmes.'

'Yes,' I replied. 'But I must pack* a suitcase* quickly. The train leaves in half an hour.'

Because I was a soldier in Afghanistan I am very good at packing quickly. Soon I was in a taxi with my suitcase, on the way to Paddington Station.

Glossary

- **detective:** person who tries to find out information about a crime
- **investigate:** find out about
- **pack:** put things in a bag or suitcase
- **patients:** people a doctor helps
- **suitcase:** bag for clothes while travelling

When I got there, Sherlock Holmes was walking up and down. He was tall and thin and he wore a long cloak• and a hat.

'Thank you very much for coming, Watson,' he said. 'It is good to have you with me. You always help me a lot. If you can find two seats on the train for us, I can buy the tickets.'

On the train, Holmes and I were the only two in the carriage•. Holmes had lots of newspapers with him. He read all the newspapers, wrote some ideas on paper and thought for a long time.

'So, Watson,' he asked. 'Do you know about the Boscombe Valley murder?'

'No, I don't. I don't read newspapers very often,' I replied.

'There isn't very much information in the London newspapers,' said Holmes. 'The Boscombe Valley murder is a simple case•, but it's also very difficult.'

'Hmmm, that sounds a little strange, Holmes,' I replied.

'But it's true,' he said. 'In this case, it looks very bad for the son of the murdered man. The police think he – the son – is the murderer. Listen, Watson, I'm going to tell you what I know.'

MATCH

Find and underline the words in the text linked to 'murder'. Then match.

1 murder   ☐ person killed
2 murdered man   ☐ illegal killing of a person
3 murderer   ☐ killer

Glossary

- **carriage:** (here) car of a train
- **case:** (here) event that police investigate
- **cloak:** long coat without sleeves

2 The Boscombe Valley murder

As the train continued, Holmes began:

'Boscombe Valley is in the countryside, not very far from Ross, a small town in Herefordshire, near the border• between England and Wales. Mr John Turner is a very rich man in that area. Mr Turner made a lot of money in Australia and came back to England many years ago. He owns a lot of land• and a lot of farms. He rented a farm, Hatherley Farm, to Mr Charles McCarthy, who is also back from Australia. The two men met in Australia many years ago. They were often together.

'McCarthy had one son,' Holmes continued, 'a boy of eighteen. Turner had a daughter of the same age. Both McCarthy and Turner were widowers•. They lived quiet lives. McCarthy had two servants•, a man and a girl. Turner had about six servants. So these are the facts about the two families. Now for some facts about the murder.

Glossary

- **border:** line between two countries
- **land:** countryside
- **servants:** people who do domestic work in a big house
- **widower:** man whose wife is dead

16

The Boscombe Valley Mystery

'Last Monday, on June 3rd, McCarthy left Hatherley Farm at about three in the afternoon. He walked down to the Boscombe Pool, a small lake in Boscombe Valley. McCarthy's servant knew he had an appointment to meet someone at three o'clock. He didn't come back from that appointment.'

'That's very strange,' I said.

'From Hatherley Farmhouse to the Boscombe Pool is about 400 metres,' Holmes continued, 'and two people saw Mr McCarthy as he passed by. One was an old woman. The other was William Crowder, Mr Turner's gamekeeper•. The old woman and the gamekeeper saw Mr McCarthy and they said he was walking alone. The gamekeeper saw the son, James McCarthy, following his father a few minutes later. And James McCarthy had a gun• under his arm.

- **gamekeeper:** person who looks after animals on a big piece of land

- **gun:**

17

'Also, Patience Moran, a girl of fourteen, the daughter of Mr Turner's servant, was walking in the woods. She saw Mr McCarthy and his son by the pool. They were having a big argument•. Patience said that old Mr McCarthy was shouting at his son.

'She saw the son move his hand as if to hit his father. She was very frightened•. She ran home and told her mother. Just then James McCarthy arrived at the house. He told them: "My father is lying dead in the woods, and I need help!"'

'That's terrible!' I cried.

'He was very upset,' said Holmes. 'He wasn't carrying his gun or wearing a hat. He had blood• on his right hand and blood on his coat.

'Patience and her mother followed young James McCarthy. They found old Mr McCarthy. He was dead, lying on the grass beside the Boscombe Pool. There were injuries• to his head, perhaps from a heavy object – perhaps the butt• of James McCarthy's gun? The gun was lying on the grass nearby. The police then arrested• the young man. They held an inquest•, and the inquest decided it was a murder. Those are the main facts of the case,' Holmes finished.

Glossary

- **argument:** angry fight
- **arrested:** took to the police station
- **blood:** red liquid in human body
- **butt:** the handle part of a gun
- **frightened:** scared; feeling fear
- **injuries:** places on the body where people are hurt
- **inquest:** court inquiry to find how a person died

The Boscombe Valley Mystery

'So, young James McCarthy is probably the murderer,' I said.

'Well,' said Holmes, 'it looks very bad for the young man, and it is possible that he is the murderer. But some people in the neighbourhood•, think young James McCarthy is innocent• – for example Miss Alice Turner, the daughter of Mr Turner. She asked Inspector Lestrade, from Scotland Yard police, to prove• Mr McCarthy is innocent, and Lestrade is working for Miss Turner. But he is puzzled•, and he wants my help. So, Watson, this is why we are travelling to the Boscombe Valley instead of eating our breakfasts at home.'

FACTS

Read and complete.
1. Name of murdered man: ....
2. Place of murder: ....
3. Time of murder: ....
4. Name/s of possible murderer/s: ....
   ....
5. Names of detectives working: ....
   ....

- **innocent:** (here) is not the murderer
- **neighbourhood:** local area
- **prove:** show
- **puzzled:** confused; not sure

3 James McCarthy's statement

'Holmes, 'I replied, 'the facts of the case look obvious•.'

'Watson, you mustn't always believe obvious facts,' Holmes answered, laughing. 'For example, your bedroom window is on the right-hand side•, but I don't think Mr Lestrade knows that.'

'How do *you* know that?' I asked.

'My dear Watson, I know you well. You shave• every morning, but your shaving is not so good on the left side of your face. This is because the light from the window shines• on the right side of your face, but not the left. You see, observation• is an important part of my job. It is possible that it can help the investigation. There are one or two important points in the Boscombe Valley murder case.'

'What are they?' I asked him.

'Well, one, the police arrested young James McCarthy when he returned to his home, Hatherley Farm. And two, when the police arrested him, young James McCarthy was not surprised. Some people think this means that young James McCarthy is guilty•.'

'That is not a very good reason,' I said.

'Yes, I agree,' said Holmes.

'So, what does the young man say?'

'Well, it's not good. Here, read the newspaper,' said Holmes.

He showed me the report• in the local newspaper.

Glossary

- **guilty:** opposite of innocent
- **observation:** looking carefully at things
- **obvious:** clear
- **report:** story in a newspaper
- **right-hand side:** on the right
- **shave:** remove hair from face
- **shines:** puts light onto something

THE BOSCOMBE VALLEY MURDER:
Mr James McCarthy's statement* to police.

James McCarthy: I was away from home for three days in Bristol, and returned last Monday morning, 3rd June. My father was not at home. The maid* said he was in Ross, with his servant John Cobb. Soon after I heard his carriage* outside. I looked out of the window. I saw my father get out and walk quickly out of the courtyard*. I did not know where he was going. I took my gun and walked to the Boscombe Pool. I was planning to shoot* rabbits.

On my way* I saw William Crowder, the gamekeeper, but he is wrong: I was not following my father, because I did not know that he was in front of me. When I was near the pool I heard a cry of *Coo-ee*. This was the signal* between my father and I. I ran forward. My father was standing by the pool. He was surprised to see me. Angrily, he asked me why I was there. We had a big argument, for my father was a very violent* man.

- **carriage:** (here) old fashioned transport with wheels which a horse pulls
- **courtyard:** area outside house
- **maid:** female servant
- **on my way:** as I walked there
- **shoot:** kill with a gun
- **signal:** sign, sound with special meaning
- **statement:** report to police by a person who saw something important
- **violent:** ready to fight or use physical force against people

James McCarthy continued:
I left my father and began to walk back to Hatherley Farm. But after only 150 metres I heard a horrible sound behind me. I ran back. My father was lying on the ground with injuries to his head. I dropped my gun and held him in my arms, but he died a few moments• later. I stayed with him for a long time. Then I went to the Morans' house, to ask for help. There was no one near my father when I returned. I have no idea how he got his injuries. He was not a popular man; he was cold and strict•, but I don't think he had any enemies•.
That is all I know.

The Coroner•: Did your father speak to you before he died?

James McCarthy: He said a few words, something about a rat, I think.

The Coroner: What did he mean•?

James McCarthy: I don't know.

The Coroner: Why were you and your father arguing?

James McCarthy: I don't want to say.

The Coroner: I'm sorry, but I must ask you again.

James McCarthy: It's impossible for me to say. It was nothing to do with the murder.

The Coroner: The court must decide that, not you. But it doesn't help if you don't answer my questions.

James McCarthy: Again, I must say no.

Glossary

- **coroner:** person who decides how someone died
- **enemies:** people who are against you
- **mean:** want to say
- **moments:** seconds
- **strict:** hard; severe

The Coroner: And the cry of *Coo-ee* was a signal between you and your father?
James McCarthy: Yes, it was.
The Coroner: Why did your father say *Coo-ee* before he saw you? Did he not know you were back from Bristol?
James McCarthy: I don't know.
The Coroner: Did you see anything strange when you found the body of your father?
James McCarthy: Yes. There was something on the ground. I think it was grey in colour, a coat or cloak perhaps. I turned away and when I looked again, it was gone.
The Coroner: How far from the body was it?
James McCarthy: About twelve metres.
The Coroner: And how far from the woods?
James McCarthy: Also about twelve metres.
The Coroner: Then perhaps someone took it when you weren't looking?
James McCarthy: Yes, perhaps.

'I see,' I said as I read the newspaper, 'the coroner is not happy with young James McCarthy. He thinks it is strange that his father shouted *Coo-ee* before he saw him. He also thinks it is strange he refused to say why he argued with his father. And then his father's dying words, something about a rat? What does that mean? It doesn't look good for young James McCarthy.'

Holmes laughed softly to himself.

'So, Watson,' he said, 'both you and the coroner are against young James McCarthy. This is because he talked about a rat, and a strange grey cloak. As for me, I believe young James McCarthy.'

BELIEVE
Do you believe obvious facts?
Do you often ask questions?
Tell a friend.

4 We meet Miss Alice Turner

We arrived at the pretty little town of Ross at about four o'clock. A small, thin man with a face like a ferret° was waiting for us. It was Lestrade, the police inspector from Scotland Yard. We all got into a carriage and drove to the Hereford Arms, our hotel.

As we were drinking tea in the hotel Lestrade laughed. He said:

'This murder case is clear and obvious. If you read the newspaper you can see that James McCarthy is the murderer. But Miss Turner wants your help, Holmes. I told her again and again there is nothing you can do. But, goodness°, here is the young lady now.'

Suddenly a beautiful young woman ran into the room. She had dark blue eyes and pink cheeks. She was very upset.

'Oh, Mr Sherlock Holmes!' she cried. 'Thank you very much for coming. I know that James didn't murder his father. I know it, and I want you to know this from the start, too. James and I grew up° together and I know him very well. He is very gentle°. He is not a murderer.'

'I hope to free him, Miss Turner,' said Sherlock Holmes. 'I am doing all that I can.'

'But you read the report in the newspapers,' she replied. 'Do you have any ideas about the case? Do you think James is innocent?'

'I think it is very likely°,' answered Holmes.

Glossary

- **ferret:** animal with a thin, pointed face
- **gentle:** calm; not violent
- **goodness:** exclamation showing surprise
- **grew up:** went from babies to adults
- **likely:** probably true

The Boscombe Valley Mystery

'There, now!' she cried. She turned her head and looked at Lestrade. 'Listen to that! Mr Holmes thinks James is innocent! He gives me hope.'

Lestrade shrugged• his shoulders. 'I think Mr Holmes is a little quick to decide that,' he said.

'But he is right. Oh! I know that he is right,' cried Miss Turner. 'James didn't murder his father. And he can't say why he argued with his father. He can't say, because the argument was about me.'

Holmes looked surprised. 'About you, Miss Turner? In what way?' he asked.

'I'm going to tell you,' said Miss Turner. 'James and his father often had arguments about me. Mr McCarthy wanted James to marry me. James and I love each other; but of course we are young and it is early for marriage. So James argued with his father a lot about this.'

'And what about your father, Mr Turner?' asked Holmes. 'Did he want you to marry James?'

'No, he didn't,' she replied. 'It was Mr McCarthy's idea.' She blushed• as Holmes looked at her.

'Thank you for this information,' he said. 'Can I see your father if I come to your house tomorrow?'

- **blushed:** went red in the face
- **shrugged:** moved shoulders up and down to show it wasn't important

27

'No, I am sorry, you can't; the doctor won't agree. My father is very ill in bed. The murder of Mr McCarthy shocked him. Mr McCarthy was his friend when they were in Victoria, Australia together.'

'Aha•! In Victoria! That is important,' said Holmes.

'Yes, they worked at the goldmines• there,' said Miss Turner.

'Yes, at the goldmines, where Mr Turner made a lot of money and became a very rich man,' said Holmes.

'Yes, certainly,' agreed Miss Turner.

'Thank you, Miss Turner. That is very helpful,' replied Holmes.

Miss Turner continued, 'Oh, if you go to the prison• to see James, please tell him that I know he is innocent. Please give me news tomorrow if you see him.'

'Of course, Miss Turner,' said Holmes.

'I must go home now, for Father is very ill,' she said. 'Goodbye.'

She ran out of the room and got into her carriage.

INFORMATION

What is the word for 'information' in your language? How is it different/similar to the word in English?

Glossary

- **Aha!:** exclamation to show you suddenly understand something
- **goldmines:** large holes in the ground where people look for gold
- **prison:** building for people who the police think are guilty

5 Holmes and Lestrade take the night train

'I am ashamed of• you, Holmes,' said Lestrade after a few minutes' silence. 'Why are you giving Miss Turner false hope•? I think it's cruel•.'

'I think I can free James McCarthy,' said Holmes. 'Can we go to the prison and see him now?'

'Yes, but only you and I can go,' replied Lestrade.

'Then I would like to go now. Can we take a train to Hereford and see him tonight?'

'Certainly,' answered Lestrade.

'Then let's go,' said Holmes. He turned to me. 'Sorry, Watson, only two people can go. I know it's boring for you, but I'm going to be back in a few hours.'

I walked down to the railway station with Holmes and Lestrade, and then continued through the streets of the little town of Ross. Finally I returned to our hotel. In my room I sat on the sofa and tried to read a novel•. The story was not very exciting. I was thinking about the mystery of the Boscombe Valley murder. Finally I threw my book on the floor. I thought and thought for a long time.

STORY

Is this story exciting?
Do you want to continue reading?
Why? Tell a friend.

- **ashamed of:** feel upset about how someone is behaving
- **cruel:** bad; horrible
- **false hope:** not a real possibility
- **novel:** book which contains a story

These were my thoughts about the mystery.

If young James McCarthy's story was true, something terrible happened after he left his father. And it happened before Mr McCarthy heard his father's screams•. That's when he ran back and saw his father dead on the ground. What was it? Perhaps there was some more information in the paper about old Mr McCarthy's injuries? I opened the newspaper again, and found a report of the inquest.

The newspaper said that Mr McCarthy had injuries to his head. Perhaps the murderer hit his head with a large heavy object. Perhaps the murderer hit Mr McCarthy from behind. Maybe Holmes needs to know about this, I thought. Then there were the dying man's words about a rat.

What did that mean? Was he trying to say the name of the murderer? But what was it?

I thought for a long time to find an answer. And then there was the grey cloak. Young James McCarthy saw it when he stood up. Did it belong to the murderer? Maybe he dropped it when he killed Mr McCarthy? And perhaps he came back for it while young James McCarthy was next to the body of his father. What a mystery! I was not surprised that Lestrade was puzzled. I was puzzled, too. But I knew Sherlock Holmes very well and he was sure that young James McCarthy was innocent.

• **screams:** loud cries

6 Holmes is back with a story

Sherlock Holmes returned very late that night. He came back alone, as Lestrade was staying at another hotel in Ross.

'I saw young James McCarthy,' Holmes said.

'And what did he tell you?' I asked him.

'Nothing,' Holmes replied.

'Nothing at all?' I continued.

'No, Watson. I thought perhaps James McCarthy knew the name of his father's murderer. But now I don't think he does. James McCarthy is not a very intelligent young man. But he is good looking, and I think he is a sensible• man.'

'I am surprised he does not want to marry Miss Turner. She is a beautiful young lady,' I said.

'Well, Watson, in fact James McCarthy is in love with• Miss Turner. He wants to marry her, but he can't,' replied Holmes.

'That's terrible!' I cried. 'Why?'

'Two years ago, when James was younger, he married a barmaid• in Bristol,' said Holmes. 'No one knows about this marriage. James is in love with Miss Turner and he wants to marry her, but he knows it is impossible.

James' father wanted him to marry Miss Turner, too. So, when he asked James about Miss Turner at the Boscombe Pool, James shouted at him and they argued. James' father didn't know anything about his other marriage and he didn't know that his son was in Bristol. Remember that, Watson. It is important,' said Holmes.

'I see,' I replied.

Glossary

- **barmaid:** woman who works in a bar or a pub
- **in love with:** loves; has romantic feelings for
- **sensible:** not stupid

The Boscombe Valley Mystery

Holmes continued: 'But something good happened in the end. The barmaid read the newspaper and saw that James McCarthy was in serious trouble• with the police. So she left him. She wrote him a letter: in the letter, she told James she already had a husband before she married him. He didn't know about this. So they are not married after all! Young James McCarthy is very happy.'

'But if young James McCarthy is innocent,' I asked, 'who murdered old Mr McCarthy?'

'Ah! Who? There are two important points here. One, old Mr McCarthy had an appointment with someone at the pool, and it was not his son, for his son was away. And two, the murdered man cried *Coo-ee* before he knew that his son was back. Those are the two important points of this case,' replied Holmes.

JAMES McCARTHY

Write a list of all the things we know about James McCarthy.
Compare your list with a friend.

• **serious trouble:** a very bad situation

7 Lestrade gets angry

There was no rain that night. In the morning it was sunny and there were no clouds in the sky. At nine o'clock Lestrade called for us in the carriage. We left for Hatherley Farm and the Boscombe Pool.

'I have some bad news for you this morning,' said Lestrade. 'Old Mr Turner is very ill; in fact he is dying.'

'I see. Is Mr Turner an elderly• man?' asked Holmes.

'No,' replied Lestrade. 'He's about sixty years old; but he's not in good health. The murder of Mr McCarthy was a big shock to him. Mr Turner was an old friend of Mr McCarthy's, and he was very kind to him. Mr McCarthy lived at Hatherley Farm rent-free•.'

'Really? That's interesting,' said Holmes.

'Oh, yes! Mr Turner helped Mr McCarthy in a hundred ways. People say Mr Turner was very good to him,' continued Lestrade.

'Really!' said Holmes. 'But it's strange that Mr McCarthy wants his son to marry Mr Turner's daughter. She's a very rich young lady and young James McCarthy has no money.'

He continued, 'And it's strange too because we know Mr Turner didn't like the idea. Miss Turner told us this. So perhaps that tells us something.'

- **elderly:** very old
- **rent-free:** not paying any money to live there

The Boscombe Valley Mystery

'Well, well, here we go. Mr Sherlock Holmes and his crazy ideas,' said Lestrade, winking• at me. 'I don't understand the facts, Holmes, but you are full of your crazy ideas.'

'You are right, Lestrade,' said Holmes. 'You don't understand the facts.'

Lestrade got angry then. 'Well, I understand one fact which you cannot understand, Holmes,' he replied.

'What is that?' asked Holmes.

'The fact is,' Lestrade continued, 'that young James McCarthy killed old Mr McCarthy. All other ideas are rubbish•.'

Holmes laughed. 'Well, let's see,' he said. 'But look, here's Hatherley Farm on the left.'

> ## WINK
> Can you wink?
> Why do people wink at each other?
> Tell a friend.

• **rubbish:** stupid; wrong   • **winking:** closing one eye

8 Holmes follows the trail

Hatherley Farm was a pretty house with grey walls. But the curtains were closed and no smoke• came from the chimney•. The maid opened the door to us. Holmes asked to see Mr McCarthy's boots – the boots he was wearing when he died. The maid showed them to us. Holmes also asked to see young James McCarthy's boots. Holmes measured the boots very carefully from seven or eight different points. Then he asked the maid to show him the courtyard. From the courtyard we all followed the path• to the Boscombe Pool.

Sherlock Holmes was a different person when he was following a trail• like this. To many people, Holmes was a quiet and logical• detective. But now he was a different person. His face was dark red. His eyebrows were like two black lines, his eyes were shining•, his shoulders hunched•, his lips were together. He was like an animal hunting• for its food.

DIFFERENT PERSON

Do you sometimes become a different person?
Why, when and how? Tell a friend.

Glossary

- **chimney:**

- **hunched:** bent over; rounded
- **hunting:** looking for
- **logical:** sensible; with clear ideas

- **path:** small road for walking
- **shining:** bright, when you are excited
- **smoke:** black or grey gas from a fire
- **trail:** series of signs left by something

37

Holmes was thinking carefully, so he did not hear when I asked a question. And then he replied with one word in an angry voice. He walked along the path quickly and silently through the grass, and through the woods to the Boscombe Pool. The ground was wet and there were many footprints•.

The footprints were on the path and also on both sides of the pool. Sometimes Holmes walked in front, sometimes he stopped, and once he suddenly turned and walked onto the grass. Lestrade and I walked behind him. Lestrade was silent and angry but I watched Holmes with interest. I knew Holmes well and I was sure that he had a plan.

Glossary

- **footprints:** marks on the ground from a person's feet

9 A murderer's footprints

The Boscombe Pool was between Hatherley Farm and the rich Mr Turner's private land. The pool was about fifty metres wide. On the other side of the pool were woods and Mr Turner's big house. On the Hatherley Farm side of the pool there were also woods. There was also a long area of wet ground six metres wide, between the edge of the woods and the pool. This was where the police found Mr McCarthy's body. Lestrade showed us the exact place. The ground was very wet, and the mark of the body was still there. Holmes looked at it very carefully. He found many other things to look at on the grass. He ran round and round, like a dog following a trail.

Then Holmes turned to Lestrade.

'Why did you go into the pool?' he asked the detective.

'To look for the murder weapon•,' said Lestrade. 'But Holmes, how did you know I went into the pool?'

'Oh, it was easy! I can see your footprints there,' said Holmes. 'I know it was you, because your left foot is twisted•.

'But there are three tracks• here of the same feet,' Holmes continued. He took out a magnifying glass• and lay on his cloak to look at the ground talking to himself all the time.

'These are James McCarthy's feet,' said Holmes. 'Twice he was walking, and once he was running fast. I know this because the soles• of the feet have deep marks, but the heels do not. So James McCarthy's story is true: he ran when he saw his father on the ground. Then here are the father's feet as he walked up and down.'

Lestrade looked at me and back at Holmes again.

'What's this, then?' continued Holmes, still talking to himself. 'It is the butt of the gun as the son stood and listened. And this? Ha, ha! What have we here? Tiptoes•! Tiptoes! Square, too, quite unusual boots! They come, they go, they come again – of course, that was when the murderer came back for the grey cloak. Now where did the footsteps come from?'

Glossary

- **magnifying glass:**
- **soles:** undersides of feet or shoes
- **tiptoes:** on the ends of the toes
- **tracks:** marks on the ground
- **twisted:** curved or bent; not straight
- **weapon:** object for killing or hurting people

Holmes ran up and down, sometimes losing the track of footprints, sometimes finding it again. He went to the woods and looked under a tall tree. Holmes followed the trail to the other side of the tree. He lay down again on his front with a little cry of happiness. 'Yes!' he cried. He stayed there for a long time. He turned over• the leaves and twigs•, and he collected something in an envelope and put it in his pocket. He looked at the ground through his magnifying glass, and also at the bark• of the tree. There was a sharp• stone lying on the ground. Holmes looked at this carefully and picked it up. Then he walked along a path through the woods until he came to the road.

'This case is very interesting,' he said, returning to normal•. 'This is Moran's house. I am going to go in and talk to Moran and perhaps write a little note to him. After that, let's drive back to the hotel and have lunch. You find a taxi, I'm coming in a few minutes.'

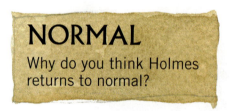

NORMAL
Why do you think Holmes returns to normal?

Glossary

- **bark:** wood on the outside of the trunk of a tree
- **normal:** (here) the Sherlock Holmes from before
- **sharp:** pointed; not round
- **turned over:** (here) looked under and over
- **twigs:** small branches from a tree

42

10 Holmes solves the mystery

About ten minutes later we took a taxi back to the small town of Ross. Holmes was still carrying the sharp stone from the woods.

'This is interesting, Lestrade,' he said, holding it out. 'The murderer killed old Mr McCarthy with this stone.'

'I don't see any marks on it,' replied Lestrade.

'No, that's because there are no marks,' answered Holmes.

'But... Holmes, how do you know this stone is the murder weapon, then?' I asked.

'The grass was short under it, so it was only there for a few days. It corresponds with• the injuries to Mr McCarthy's head. And it is the only weapon here,' Holmes answered.

WEAPON
Draw a picture of the murder weapon.

Glossary

- **corresponds with:** goes with; is the same as

The Boscombe Valley Mystery

'But what about the murderer?' asked Lestrade.

'Well,' replied Holmes. 'The murderer is a tall man, he is left-handed, and his right leg has a limp•. He wears big boots and a grey cloak. Also, he smokes Indian cigars, and he uses a cigar-holder. There are other things, but I think this is enough for now,' said Holmes.

Lestrade laughed. 'I am sorry, Holmes, but I still don't agree with you,' he said. 'Do you really think a British jury• is going to believe your crazy ideas?'

'*Nous verrons*,' answered Holmes calmly• in French. 'Let's see. You work your way, and I work my way. I'm going to be busy this afternoon, and I'm probably going back to London on the evening train.'

'But the Boscombe Valley murder case isn't finished,' said Lestrade.

'Oh yes, it is finished,' replied Holmes.

'But what about the mystery?' continued Lestrade.

'I solved the mystery,' said Holmes.

'So, who was the murderer, then?' Lestrade asked, still puzzled.

'The man I described• to you,' answered Holmes.

MURDERER

What do we know about the murderer? Write a list.

- **calmly:** slowly; without anger
- **described:** gave details of how something looked
- **jury:** twelve people who decide if a person is innocent or guilty
- **has a limp:** walks with difficulty because of injury to leg or foot

45

'But who is he?' said Lestrade again.

'It's not hard to find out,' replied Holmes. 'This isn't a big neighbourhood.'

Lestrade shrugged his shoulders. 'I am a practical man,' he said, 'and I can't go around the countryside looking for a left-handed man with a limp in his right leg. I don't want to be the joke• of Scotland Yard!'

'All right,' said Holmes quietly. 'Here we are at your hotel. Goodbye, Lestrade. I can write you a note before I leave.'

We left Lestrade, and drove to our hotel. We had lunch there. During lunch Holmes was silent and had a strange expression on his face. He looked puzzled.

SCOTLAND YARD

What do you know about Scotland Yard?
Do some research on the Internet and discuss in small groups.

- **joke:** person or thing people laugh at

11 Holmes asks Watson's advice

'Look here, Watson,' Holmes said after we finished lunch. 'Please sit down. I want to talk to you. I don't know what to do, and your advice• is important to me. You smoke your cigar while I explain.'

'Please continue,' I said, as I lit my cigar.

'Well, now, there are three important points in young James McCarthy's story. One, his father cries *Coo-ee* before he sees him. Two, he talks about a rat. I think young James McCarthy is telling the truth.'

'So why did old Mr McCarthy shout *Coo-ee* then?'

'Well, he was not shouting *Coo-ee* to his son. His son was in Bristol. It was by chance• that the son heard. The *Coo-ee* was to call the person he was meeting. But *Coo-ee* is an Australian cry, and Australians usually say it when they meet, want to attract attention or state their location. Perhaps Mr McCarthy was meeting someone from Australia at the Boscombe Pool.'

COO-EE

Can you think of a similar expression in your language? Is it used for the same or different reasons?
Discuss in small groups.

- **advice:** ideas from another person to help you decide something
- **chance:** luck; accident

The Boscombe Valley Mystery

'I see. But why did he talk about a rat, then?' I asked.

Sherlock Holmes took a piece of paper from his pocket and put it on the table.

'This is a map of Australia,' he said. He put his hand over part of the map. 'Now, Watson, what can you read there?' he asked me.

'ARAT,' I read.

'And now?' Holmes moved his hand.

'BALLARAT,' I read.

'Yes. That was the word the man said. It is a place called Ballarat. His son only heard the 'rat' part of the word. Old Mr McCarthy was trying to say where his murderer was from, the town of Ballarat.'

'That's wonderful, Holmes!' I exclaimed•.

BALLARAT

Do some research on the Internet in small groups.
What type of town is Ballarat today?
Look for information and photos.

Glossary

exclaimed: said with excitement

'Yes, it is obvious. The grey cloak is point number three. If James is telling the truth, there was a grey cloak. So from a complete mystery we now have an Australian from Ballarat with a grey cloak.'

'Brilliant!' I replied.

'And it's someone who lives nearby, as the Boscombe Pool is not open to the public. Only people from Hatherley Farm or the Turner house can go there,' said Holmes.

'Yes,' I agreed.

'Then today, when I looked at the ground I found the other details. These are the details I gave to that idiot Lestrade. You remember, the description of the murderer,' said Holmes.

'But how did you find them?' I asked.

'You know how I work. I look at the details,' Holmes replied.

DETAILS
Write down ALL the details you now know:

The Boscombe Valley Mystery

'I know you found his height from the length of his stride•,' I said. 'And you knew the size of his boots, too, from their footprints.'

'Yes, they were unusual boots,' agreed Holmes.

'But what about the limp?' I asked. 'How did you know about that?'

'The print of his left foot was very clear,' Holmes explained. 'But the print of his right foot was not. He did not put the same weight upon the right as the left. Why? Because he had a limp in his right leg.'

'But how did you know the murderer was left-handed?' I asked.

'The murderer hit Mr McCarthy's head from behind,' replied Holmes. 'He hit him on the left side of the head. Only a left-handed man can do that. The murderer was behind the tall tree when the father and son were arguing. He smoked a cigar there – I found the ash• on the ground. As you know, I once wrote a small book about the 140 different kinds of cigar, pipe and cigarette ash.'

'Holmes,' I said. 'I see what this means. You can save James McCarthy's life! This means that the murderer is…'

'Mr John Turner,' cried the hotel waiter, opening the door of the room, and showing in• a visitor.

Glossary

- **ash:** grey powder after a cigar or cigarette burns
- **showing in:** taking a person into a room
- **stride:** space between one long footstep and the next

53

12 Mr John Turner speaks

The visitor was a tall, strange man. He had a limp in his right leg and his shoulders were bent. His face was hard with a lot of lines. He looked very strong: he had huge• arms and legs. He had a long beard, grey hair, and big eyebrows. His face was calm and strong. But his skin was very white, and his lips were blue. As a doctor, it was clear to me that this man was very ill.

'Please sit down,' said Holmes kindly to him. 'You got my note?'

'Yes. You asked me to come here. You didn't want to visit me, to avoid a scandal•,' replied Mr John Turner.

'Yes,' replied Holmes. 'People often talk when Sherlock Holmes visits a house.'

'And why did you want to see me?' Mr Turner looked at Holmes with sad, tired eyes, as if he knew the answer to his question.

'I know all about McCarthy,' said Holmes.

The old man put his face in his hands. 'God help me•!' he cried.

'But I did not want young James to go to prison or die. I give you my word.'

'I am happy to hear it,' said Holmes seriously.

'I'm speaking to you now because of my daughter Alice,' continued Mr Turner. 'She loves James and she wants him to be free. Her heart is going to break• when the police arrest me.'

'Perhaps the police won't arrest you,' said Holmes.

'What?' said Mr Turner, surprised.

Glossary

- **God help me!:** exclamation when very bad things are happening to you
- **her heart is going to break:** she is going to be very upset
- **huge:** very big
- **scandal:** when a bad thing becomes public and shocks people

'I'm not the police,' said Holmes. 'I'm here because Miss Turner asked me to come, and I am working for her. We must free young James McCarthy.'

'I am dying,' said old Turner. 'My doctor says I'm going to die in a month. But I prefer to die at home, not in prison.'

Holmes sat down at the table with his pen in his hand and some papers in front of him. 'Please tell us the truth,' he said. 'I'm going to write down the facts. You're going to sign it, and Watson here is our witness•. Then I have your confession• if I need it to save young James McCarthy. I promise not to use it if I don't need to.'

'Yes,' said the old man. 'I don't know if I am going to live until the trial.• It's not important to me, but I don't want Alice to have a big shock. And now I am going to tell you my story; it happened over a period of twenty years, but I'm going to tell you in a few minutes.

'You didn't know the dead man, McCarthy,' said Mr Turner. 'He was evil•, it's true. He followed me for twenty years, and ruined• my life. I'm going to tell you how I met him.'

CONFESSION

Why does Holmes need Mr Turner's confession?
How is a confession like a story?
 Discuss in small groups.

Glossary

- **confession:** statement saying you are guilty
- **evil:** very bad
- **ruined:** made bad; spoiled
- **trial:** when a court decides if a person is guilty or innocent
- **witness:** (here) person who signs to say they heard or saw a confession

13 A murderer's story

He began his story: 'In the early 1860s we were working in goldmines in Australia. I was a young man then. I did not find any gold. Then I started to drink•, and made bad friends. I lived in the bush•, and became a robber•. I was in a gang. There were six of us. My name was Black Jack of Ballarat, and we six were the Ballarat Gang.

'One day some wagons• came carrying gold from Ballarat to Melbourne. Our gang attacked them. There were six soldiers and six of us robbers. But we took four of their bags of gold. But the soldiers killed three of our boys before we got the gold. McCarthy was the wagon-driver. I pointed my gun at his head, but I didn't kill him. I let him go•. His little eyes were watching me carefully because he wanted to remember me,' Turner continued.

'We escaped with the gold, and became rich men,' he said. 'I came back to England. I left my gang and started a new life as a quiet and good man. I bought Hatherley Farm and I tried to do good with my money. I felt bad that it was stolen•. I married, too, but my wife died. She left me with my little Alice. When I had a child I became a good person again. All was going well when McCarthy came back to England and found me.'

He was silent for a moment, then continued:

'I was in London, and I met him one day in Regent Street. He was very poor, with no coat or boots.

- **bush:** countryside in Australia
- **drink:** (here) drink a lot of alcohol; become an alcoholic
- **let him go:** freed him
- **robber:** person who steals things
- **stolen:** taken without permission
- **wagons:** vehicles for carrying goods

'"Well, Turner," he said as he touched my arm. "Me and my son are going to be your family. You're going to look after us. If you don't, I'm going to the police to tell them you were a robber in Australia."

'So,' continued Mr Turner, 'McCarthy and his son came to live near here. It was impossible to escape them, and they lived at Hatherley Farm rent-free from that time. I had no peace• from them. When I went out, McCarthy was always behind me. And when Alice grew up, McCarthy saw that I didn't want Alice to know about my life as a robber in Australia. He asked for the things he wanted, and I gave them all to him: land, money, houses. But then one day, he asked for a thing I did not want to give. He asked for Alice.'

Mr Turner closed his eyes. He drank some water and continued, 'His son James was now grown up, and so was my Alice. McCarthy knew I was very ill. He wanted all my money for his son. But I said no to the marriage. I didn't want Alice to marry a McCarthy. I said no again and again. McCarthy and I had an appointment to meet at the pool halfway• between our houses to talk about the marriage.

'When I arrived at the Boscombe Pool old McCarthy was talking to his son. So I smoked a cigar and waited behind a tree. But as I listened to McCarthy I got very angry. He wanted his son to marry my daughter. He didn't care• if Alice wanted to marry his son or not. Alice was in his power. I hated that. He was an evil man. I was dying. I knew that it was all finished for me. But my memory• and my poor Alice! I wanted to save Alice from McCarthy.

Glossary

- **didn't care:** was not interested in
- **halfway:** at a point exactly between two places
- **memory:** (here) how people remember you after you die
- **peace:** quiet; calm

The Boscombe Valley Mystery

'Yes, I did it, Mr Holmes. I killed McCarthy. I did a terrible thing, but my life was a nightmare•. I did it for Alice. I hit McCarthy with the stone as if he were an animal. He screamed and his son came back but I was already in the woods. I had to go back to get my grey cloak. I dropped it when I hit McCarthy. That is the true story, gentlemen,' finished Mr Turner.

'Well, I'm not going to judge• you,' said Holmes as the old man signed the statement.

'What are you going to do now?' asked Mr Turner.

'Because you're dying, I'm going to do nothing,' Holmes told him. 'You know that soon God is going to judge you. I'm going to keep your statement. If the judge finds James McCarthy guilty, I am going to use the statement. If not, I am not going to show it to the police. Don't worry, Mr Turner. Your secret is safe with us.'

'Goodbye, then,' said the old man sadly. 'Thank you. I can die in peace now.' He walked slowly from the room, shaking•.

'God help us!' said Holmes after a long silence. 'The poor man.'

DYING MAN

Do you agree with Holmes' decision? Why?/Why not?
Discuss in small groups.

- **judge:** give your ideas about a person after you know what they did
- **nightmare:** terrible dream
- **shaking:** making lots of small, quick movements because you are upset

Luckily, the judge found James McCarthy innocent. This was because Holmes helped James's legal representative by showing him all the problems with the case. The jury were not sure that James was guilty, so they freed him. Old Mr Turner lived for seven months after he spoke to Holmes, but he is now dead. And perhaps James and Alice can have a happy life together, because they don't know about the black cloud in their past.

After Reading

Personal Response

1 **Read each statement and circle the number that is most true for you.**

   1 = absolutely not   **5** = very much

   a) It's a good story.
      1   2   3   4   5
   b) I had no problems understanding the story.
      1   2   3   4   5
   c) I now know lots of new words.
      1   2   3   4   5
   d) The pictures helped me understand the story.
      1   2   3   4   5
   e) I want to recommend the book to a friend.

2 **Do you think Sherlock Holmes is a good detective?**

3 **Who is your favourite character in the story? Who is your least favourite character?**

4 **What is the link between Mr Charles McCarthy and Mr John Turner?**

5 **Do you like the ending? Discuss in groups.**

61

After Reading

Comprehension

1 **Are the following sentences true (T) or false (F)? Tick (✓).**

                                                                                       T   F

a) The story begins when Holmes visited Watson to ask for help with the Boscombe Valley murder. ☐ ☐

b) Holmes and Watson travelled to the Boscombe Valley on the 11:15 train from Paddington. ☐ ☐

c) Holmes told Watson that Charles McCarthy and John Turner met in Australia. ☐ ☐

d) On the day of the murder, Charles McCarthy went to the Boscombe Pool to meet someone at six o'clock. ☐ ☐

e) Two people saw his son James by the pool with a gun. ☐ ☐

f) Later James McCarthy found his father lying by the pool. He had injuries to his head. ☐ ☐

g) The police arrested James McCarthy and put him in prison. ☐ ☐

h) Alice Turner told Watson and Holmes that she did not want to marry James. ☐ ☐

i) James said he was already married to a barmaid in Bristol. ☐ ☐

j) When Holmes, Watson and Lestrade went to the pool, Holmes found footprints and other clues. ☐ ☐

k) Holmes told Lestrade that the murderer was a tall left-handed man with a limp in his right leg. ☐ ☐

l) John Turner arrived at the hotel and told Holmes and Watson that he killed Charles McCarthy, but he was dying, too. ☐ ☐

After Reading

2 In pairs answer the questions.

a) Why did James McCarthy have an argument with his father?
b) What happened after James had a big argument with his father?
c) Why did Holmes not tell the police about John Turner's confession?
d) Why could James and Alice now be together?

3 Match the two halves of the sentences.

a) When Dr Watson reads about the Boscombe Valley murder,
b) Before the murder, Patience Moran, a girl of fourteen, saw Mr McCarthy
c) On the train, Holmes tells Watson that McCarthy and Turner were both widowers,
d) James McCarthy's barmaid wife wrote him a letter to say
e) When Holmes went to the Boscombe Pool, he found
f) Holmes told Lestrade that the murderer was a tall man,
g) When old Mr McCarthy said something about a rat, he was trying to say
h) Mr Turner told Holmes and Watson that he killed McCarthy

1 ☐ she already had a husband before she married him.
2 ☐ was left-handed and had a limp in his right leg.
3 ☐ he thinks the facts of the case look obvious.
4 ☐ that he was from Ballarat in Australia.
5 ☐ footprints, cigar ash and a large stone.
6 ☐ because he was evil and he wanted to save Alice from him.
7 ☐ and his son having a big argument by the pool.
8 ☐ and each had one child.

After Reading

Characters

1 Complete the sentences with an adjective.

> beautiful   puzzled   rich   sensible   logical   thin

a) A small .... man with a face like a ferret was waiting for us.
b) A .... young woman ran into the room. She had dark blue eyes and pink cheeks.
c) 'He is not a very intelligent young man. But he is good-looking and I think he is ....'
d) To many people, he was a quiet and .... detective. But now he was a different person.
e) I was .... by the Boscombe Valley murder.
f) He was a .... man. He made a lot of money in Australia.

2 Match the sentences from Exercise 1 to the correct characters.

Sherlock Holmes

Inspector Lestrade

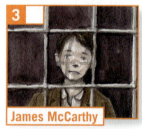
James McCarthy

Dr Watson

Mr John Turner

Miss Alice Turner

After Reading

3 Complete the conversation between Sherlock Holmes and Inspector Lestrade. Circle the correct word.

'It's strange / good that Mr McCarthy wants his son to marry Mr Turner's daughter,' said Holmes. 'She's a very rich / poor young lady and James McCarthy has no / lots of money. Perhaps that tells us something.'
'Well, well, here we go, Mr Sherlock Holmes and his crazy / wonderful ideas,' said Lestrade, winking / shouting at me. 'I understand / don't understand the facts, Holmes, but you are full of your crazy ideas.'
'You are right / wrong, Lestrade,' said Holmes. 'You don't understand the facts.'

**4 Compare Sherlock Holmes and Inspector Lestrade. What are they like? How do they work? What do you know about them? What do we learn about them in this story?
What does the conversation in Exercise 3 tell you about them? Share your ideas with a partner.**

5 Write a dialogue of the argument between Mr Charles McCarthy and his son by the Boscombe Pool before the murder. Act it out with a partner.

6 Do you feel sorry for John Turner, the murderer? Why? Why not?

After Reading

Plot and Theme

1. **What happens in the story? Put the events in the correct order.**

   a) ☐ Holmes said that he was going to do nothing because Mr Turner was dying.

   b) ☐ The next morning Holmes, Watson and Lestrade went to the Boscombe Pool. Holmes looked for clues.

   c) ☐ Mr Turner said that he met McCarthy when he was a robber in Australia.

   d) ☐ Turner says he killed McCarthy with a stone, because he wanted to save Alice from him.

   e) ☐ On the train, Watson read about the case.

   f) ☐ Holmes and Lestrade visited James McCarthy in prison. He told them he wanted to marry Miss Turner but was already married to a barmaid.

   g) ☐ Holmes then told Lestrade the murderer was a tall, left-handed man with a limp in his right leg.

   h) ☐ Watson and Holmes travelled by train from London to the Boscombe Valley to investigate a murder.

   i) ☐ Miss Alice Turner came to the hotel and talked to Holmes.

   j) ☐ The judge decided James McCarthy was innocent after Holmes helped.

   k) ☐ Lestrade didn't agree and said he didn't want to be the joke of Scotland Yard.

   l) ☐ Mr John Turner came to the hotel.

After Reading

2 Match the pictures with the descriptions. Then choose your favourite part of the story and say why you like it.

a) Watson and Holmes on the train
b) Miss Turner's visit
c) Holmes looking for clues
d) Holmes's argument with Lestrade
e) Mr John Taylor's confession

3 Fill in the missing letters to find the themes from the story.

a) F _ M _ L _
b) M _ N E _
c) C R I M _
d) A U _ T R _ L I A
e) _ A R _ I A G E

R M I Y A Y A S O E

4 Work with a partner. Choose one of the themes and say how it is important in the story.

67

After Reading

Language

1 Read the definitions of these words in the story. Complete the word. There is one space for each letter.

a) A paper with a short message   t _ _ _ _ _ _ _
b) A long coat without sleeves   c _ _ _ _
c) A story in a newspaper   r _ _ _ _ _
d) Twelve people who decide if a person is innocent or guilty   j _ _ _
e) Marks on the ground from a person's feet   f _ _ _ _ _ _ _ _ _

2 Match the sentence halves.

a) ☐ Watson was eating breakfast when
b) ☐ Holmes and Watson were drinking tea in their hotel when
c) ☐ As they were travelling by train to the Boscombe Valley
d) ☐ When James McCarthy and his father had a big argument
e) ☐ Mr John Turner arrived at the hotel

1 Miss Turner arrived to speak to them.
2 Holmes showed Watson a report about the murder in the newspaper.
3 a telegram came from Sherlock Holmes.
4 when Holmes was telling Watson he'd written a book about ash.
5 John Turner was listening to them behind a tree.

After Reading

3 Put the words in the correct order to make questions.

   a) was / murderer / who / the?
   ....

   b) Holmes / why / not / give / did / Turner's / the / confession / police / to / ?
   ....

   c) did / their / argument / have / James / and / where / father / his / big / ?
   ....

   d) Charles / when / Turner / did / John / first / McCarthy / meet / ?
   ....

   e) what / James / when / him / was / Boscombe / Pool / with / went / he / to / carrying / the / ?
   ....

4 Ask and answer the questions in Exercise 3 with a partner.

5 Complete the sentences with *and*, *so*, *but* or *because*.

   a) Holmes .... Lestrade went to visit James McCarthy in prison.

   b) Holmes thought James McCarthy was innocent, ... Lestrade thought he was guilty.

   c) John Turner killed Charles McCarthy .... he wanted to save his daughter Alice from him.

   d) James wanted to marry Alice, but he knew it was impossible, ... he shouted at his father when his father asked him.

69

After Reading

Exit Test

1 Listen and tick (✓) the correct picture.

a) 1 ☐    2 ☐

b) 1 ☐    2 ☐

c) 1 ☐    2 ☐

d) 1 ☐    2 ☐

After Reading

K 2 **Read the sentences. Choose the best word.**

a) After he .... Holmes's telegram, Watson was soon in a taxi with his suitcase.

1 sent   **2** wrote   **3** got

b) Holmes .... Watson that McCarthy and Turner were both widowers.

1 shouted   **2** told   **3** cried

c) Before Mr McCarthy died people saw him and his son .... an argument.

1 having   **2** doing   **3** explaining

d) James McCarthy told the coroner that his father was a .... man.

1 violent   **2** gentle   **3** sensible

e) Before Mr McCarthy died he said .... about a rat.

1 anything   **2** nothing   **3** something

f) Holmes told Lestrade that the murder .... was a stone.

1 knife   **2** weapon   **3** gun

g) The murderer was a tall, left-handed man who .... Indian cigars.

1 smoked   **2** sold   **3** found

h) When old McCarthy was talking to his son, Turner waited .... a tree.

1 on top of **2** behind   **3** in front of

i) Luckily the .... decided James McCarthy was innocent.

1 judge   **2** police   **3** detective

After Reading

Project

AUSTRALIA IN THE 20TH CENTURY

1 In the story, Charles McCarthy and John Turner worked in the gold mines in Australia. Work in groups and find information to answer the following questions. Use the Internet to help you.
- What was Australia like in the early 20th century?
- Where were the gold mines?
- Where did people come from to find gold?

AUSTRALIA TODAY

2 How much do you know about Australia today? Work in groups and find information about the following aspects. Use the Internet to help you.
- Big cities
- Animals and birds
- Food and drink
- Natural parks
- Aborigines (native people)
- National customs